Usborne

Magical Stories
for
Little Children

Usborne

Magical Stories
for
Little Children

Contents

The Wish Fish

This is a story about

Bob, a fisherman,

Bet, his wife,

and one very special fish.

Bob and Bet lived in a tumble-down cottage by the sea.

They loved living by the sea – and they loved fish.

Early each morning, Bob set out in his creaky old boat.
He fished all day long.

Some days,
the fish he caught were
enormous...

But, on other days,
they were only
teeny, tiny, tiddlers.

Then, one glorious day, he caught...

... a stunningly, stupendously magical fish!

He popped it in a jar and rowed home,
as fast as he could.

"Hello," said the fish. "If you let me go,
I'll grant you three wishes."

"I wish we were rich,"
Bob said, at once.

With a fizz and a crackle
and a shower of stars...
Bob and Bet *were* rich.

Their cottage was transformed into a mansion.
Bob's creaky old boat became a magnificent ship.

"This is fun!" said Bob.
"I wish we were richer..."

In the blink of an eye, Bet was wearing a glittering tiara and dazzling jewels.

"Yippee!" yelled Bob, juggling bags of gold.

"We still have one more wish," said Bet. "I wish...
I wish we were the richest couple in the whole wide world."

27

"What a greedy pair!" said the fish.

Bob and Bet's riches popped around them.
They had asked for too much and now...

...they were left with nothing.

The Magic Pear Tree

Shen lived all by himself, in a little house with a huge garden.

In the garden stood a tree covered in sweet, golden pears.

32

There were far too many pears for Shen.
But he didn't want to share them.

"I'll sell them at the market for lots of money!" he said.

Go away!

"Pears, sweet pears!"
Shen called out, at
the bustling market.

A beggar walked
by. "Please may
I have a pear?"

Shen frowned.
"Can you pay?"

The beggar shook his
head. "I don't have any
money," he sighed.

"Then go away!"
shouted Shen.

How mean!

A kind woman
heard Shen shouting.

36

"Can't you spare *one* pear?" she asked Shen.
"That man is hungry and you have plenty."

"NO!" yelled Shen.

"Then I'll buy a pear and give it to him myself," the woman said.

You're very kind.

"Thank you," said the beggar.

He gobbled up the pear
– skin, stalk and all.

A moment later, he
spat out the seeds.

The beggar wiped his lips and smiled at the woman.
"Now it's my turn to give *you* a pear."

"Aha!" cried Shen. "So you
DO have some money!"

"No," said the beggar.

The woman looked puzzled.
"So how will you get another pear?"

The beggar smiled.
"I'll show you," he said.
"Just watch..."

A curious crowd joined Shen and the woman as the beggar began to dig.

First, he made
a little hole.
Then he popped
the pear seeds into it.

The beggar looked up. "Now I need some hot water or tea," he said.

A tea-seller passed him a steaming teapot.

The beggar poured hot tea into the hole. Swirls of steam billowed up...

Suddenly, the crowd gasped. "Look, a shoot!"

45

The shoot grew and grew.

It's magic!

It grew into a tree, with gleaming leaves and shining golden pears.

Yum, yum...

The beggar plucked a pear and gave it to the woman.
He picked pear after pear, until the tree was bare.

48

Everyone got one – even selfish Shen.

When he had finished eating,
Shen glanced around.

Oh no!

To his horror, all his pears had gone!
And their wooden box was chopped to pieces.

"It was a trick," he yelled. "Those pears the beggar picked –
they were mine!"

"The beggar turned my box into a tree by magic, and then he *stole* my pears!"

That thieving beggar!

To Shen's dismay, the crowd laughed.

"Next time, perhaps you'll be less selfish," everyone said.

The Golden Goose

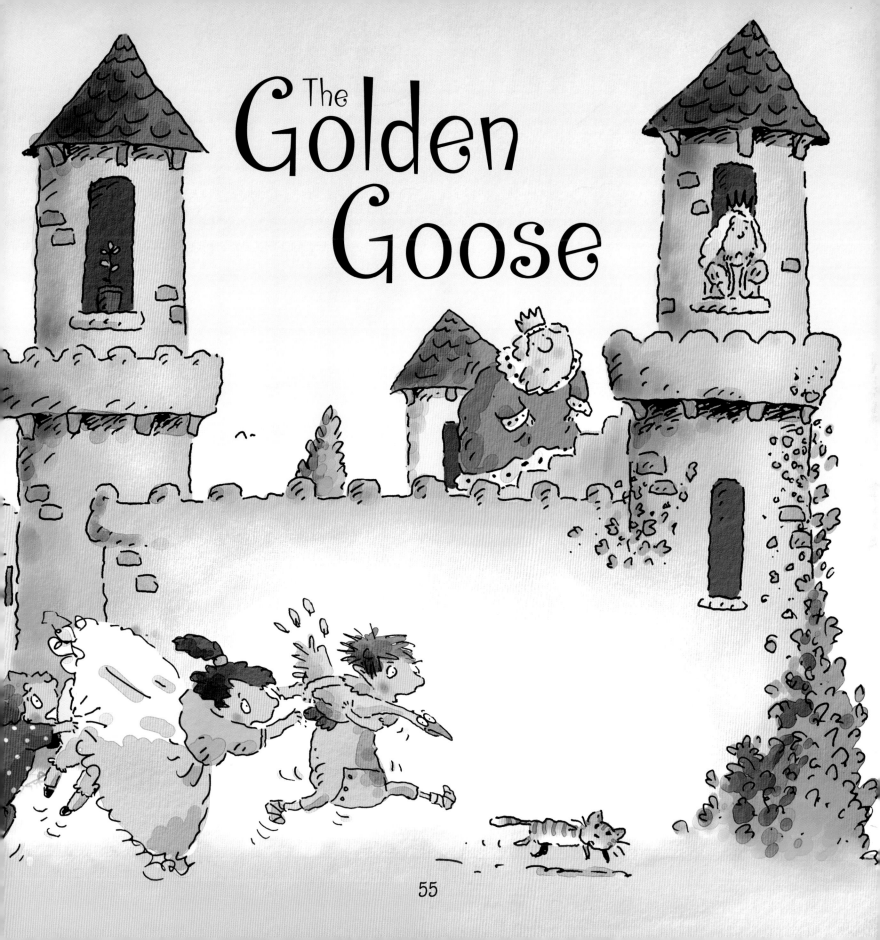

There was once a woodcutter, who lived deep in a forest with his three sons.

Ronald was strong.

Donald was
handsome.

And Billy...
was just Billy.

One day, the woodcutter
woke up feeling terrible.

"Oh dear," he groaned.
"Now who will chop
the wood?"

Billy chopped wood all morning. He had just sat down to lunch when...

POP! A little old man appeared.

"Please can you spare some food?" he begged.

"Here!" said Billy. "Have as much as you like."

"Scrumptious!" said the little old
man, munching happily.

"Now, cut down that tree
and see what happens."

Billy put his saw to the tree. With a shuddering creak, it split in two.

CREAK!

There, in the trunk, sat a *golden goose!*

"Wait until Dad sees this!" said Billy.

But he couldn't remember
the way home.

By nightfall, he was
hopelessly lost.

"We'll have to stay at
an inn overnight," he
told the goose.

"That's a very fine goose!" said the innkeeper,
as Billy strode in.

"Thank you," said Billy, and booked a room.

That night, the innkeeper's daughters crept into Billy's room.

"Look at all those lovely golden feathers," whispered the eldest.

"I'm sure he won't miss one."

But the second she touched
the goose...

...she stuck fast!

Her two sisters
rushed to help...

...and then they
were all stuck.

Billy leaped out of bed and
tugged at the goose. He was
as stuck as the girls.

"Oh well," he sighed. "We'll
just have to stay stuck." And
he went back to bed.

68

The next morning, Billy set off
with his goose...

...with the three girls
following behind.

"Girls!" screeched the innkeeper's wife. "Come back here at once!" She reached out to grab her youngest daughter...

...and Zap! She stuck to her like glue.

"Don't worry dear," called the innkeeper. "I've got you!"
He grabbed his wife...

...and Zap!
He stuck as
fast as the rest.

"Oh dear," said Billy.
"You'll ALL have to
come home with me."

Soon, Billy was
lost again.

After a while,
they came to a castle.

Now, in this castle lived a princess who had never, ever smiled. Not once. This made her father very sad.

But when she saw
the innkeeper...

his wife...

and the
three girls...

all following behind
Billy and his goose...

73

...she started
to smile.

Then she grinned.

Ha! Ha! HA!

And then she
laughed out loud.

"At last!" cried the king. "Young man, as a reward would you like to marry my daughter?"

"Yes please," said Billy.

"Yippee!" said the princess.

"Excellent!" said the king. "You shall marry today. We will send for your family at once."

There was a **POP!** and the
little old man appeared.

He waggled his walking stick in the air...

...and everyone came un-stuck.

Billy and the princess lived happily ever after – and no one ever touched the golden goose again.

The Three Wishes

Once upon a time, in a faraway land, a poor man named Ned lived with his wife, Nat.

Ned and Nat were very poor and they never had enough to eat.

82

They were so hungry, their tummies
rumbled and grumbled.

One morning, Ned was working in the fields, when he heard the softest cry.

A fairy was trapped in some hay.

Help!

"Dear me!" said Ned, and he gently unhooked her wings.

"Thank you, oh thank you!" gasped the fairy.

She hopped onto Ned's hand, lighter than a feather.
"Please let me give you three wishes."

"Thank *you*!" said Ned.

And his mind filled with thoughts
of all the wishes he could make.

Too excited to work,
Ned raced home.

88

"Nat! Nat! We have three wishes!" he shouted.

"Really?" said Nat, running down the path to meet him.

Back in their cottage, Nat looked thoughtful.
"This is incredible, Ned," she said.
"Ooh! I wish for..."

"A sausage!"
said Ned.

Ting!

"A sausage?" demanded Nat. "You wished for a **sausage**? You silly old fool!"

"But I'm hungry!"

Ned was furious. How dare Nat be so rude to him?

"Silly am I?" he said. "We'll see who's the silly one.
I wish the sausage was on the end of your nose!"

Ting!

The sausage flew from the plate and stuck to Nat's nose.

Nat
was
livid!

Even Ned looked a
little shocked.

"Ned!" Nat wailed.
"Help!"

They had one wish left. Ned sighed.
"I wish the sausage was off your nose," he said.

Ting!

And it was. Nat stroked her nose in relief.

"Now we have no wishes," she said.

Ned grinned. "But we still have the sausage!"

The Magic Porridge Pot

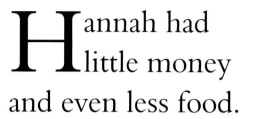

H annah had little money and even less food.

Sigh!

But whatever she had, she always shared.

One day, Hannah was out
for a walk, when she saw
some bees.

"Aha!" thought Hannah.
"Bees mean honey."

As Hannah ate the honey,
an old woman hobbled up,
swinging an empty pot.

"Would you like some honey?" asked Hannah.

"Ooh, yes please!" said the woman.

"It sounds perfect for my porridge."

"Porridge? What porridge?" Hannah asked.

The woman smiled.
"Watch!"

Cook pot, cook!

With a sizzle of magic,
steaming porridge filled
the pot.

Stop pot, stop!

Then, just as quickly,
it stopped.

They each ate a bowl of delicious porridge drizzled with sweet, sticky honey.

"Would you like the pot?" the woman said. "Remember the magic words and you'll never go hungry again."

Mmmm!

Mmmm!

From then on, Hannah had plenty to eat. She had porridge for breakfast...

porridge for lunch...

and porridge for supper.

111

One evening, a greedy boy smelled the porridge.

Mmm, what's that?

He followed his nose to Hannah's cottage.

112

He saw the pot start to fill with porridge...

...but Hannah drew the curtains, so he didn't see it stop.

The boy waited for
Hannah to go to bed.

Then he tiptoed in, grabbed the
pot and ran all the way home.

He couldn't wait to shout the magic words.

Cook pot, cook!

With a sizzle of magic, the pot filled with porridge. It got fuller... and fuller...

"That's enough," said the
boy. "You can stop now."

What a mess...

But the pot didn't stop.

Puddles of porridge poured onto the floor.

"That's too much," cried the boy. "Stop, I tell you!"

Uh oh...

But the pot didn't stop.

It filled the room
with a gloopy sea
of porridge.

Soon, porridge was pouring out of the doors and windows.

"*Please* stop!" begged the boy.

120

But the pot didn't stop.

The boy sploshed out
into the night.

"Stop, stop, STOP!"
he yelled. "I'll drown
in porridge!"

But *still* the pot didn't stop.

In her bedroom, Hannah sniffed. "That smells like porridge!" she thought.

She raced outside. Porridge was flooding down the street.

Oh no! It must be the pot.

124

Hannah shouted the magic words.

Stop pot, stop!

And, at last, the pot stopped. The greedy boy was saved.

He couldn't return Hannah's pot fast enough. And he never stole anything again.

About the stories

The Wish Fish

The Wish Fish is based on an old folk tale. It is popular in many countries, from Germany to India. The story was probably first told in Russia, where it is known as *The Golden Fish*.

The Magic Pear Tree

The Magic Pear Tree is a traditional tale from China. In some versions of the story, the beggar is a Buddhist monk.

The Golden Goose

The Golden Goose was first written down by two brothers, Jacob and Wilhelm Grimm, about two hundred years ago. They lived in Germany and collected lots of folk tales.